LONGHORN

HARD TIME, BOOK 2

EREC STEBBINS

TWICE PI PRESS

Only one thing is impossible for God: to find any sense in any copyright law on the planet.—Mark Twain

Hard Time, Book 2: Longhorn. Copyright © 2018 Erec Stebbins

Published 2018 by Twice Pi Press, erecstebbinsbooks.com

Cover design by Erec Stebbins © 2018. Edited by Michael Matheson.

ePub ISBN-13: 978-1-942360-37-7

Kindle ISBN-13: 978-1-942360-38-4

Paperback ISBN-13: 978-1-942360-39-1

Content Guide

This novel contains depictions and references to events and ideas that some will find disturbing, possibly including, but not limited to, monsters, gore, death, torture, captivity, severe illness, pain, fear, medical procedures, and violence. There is also profanity and strong language, the challenging of some accepted norms, and the questioning of different kinds of authority, religious and secular. The book may also contain religion, Oxford commas, and an unnecessary number of tpyos and, grammer misteaks. Readers are asked to prepare accordingly.

1

BONES

The man screamed.

Agony drove fingers to shield his eyes from the bloated red star. Oozing blisters across his hands and face crusted with sand from the entombing wasteland. Red drifts buried his shins in the hot wind.

A shirt hung over his head to block the scalding crimson rays, sunglasses feeble to quench the acid in his eyes from dust and light. His sleeves were yanked to cover every possible patch of skin.

He held fast like a fetus, balled and concealing anything organic from the elements. Footprints extended behind him, across endless dunes of red, erased by wind and shifting grains in the distance. His body shook with ragged and desperate breaths.

A proud dome rose at a great distance, the monochrome red reflecting mercilessly from its surface. Its measure was unfathomable to scorched eyes. Its location shrouded in heat and pain, waves of atmosphere distorting the space between. It could be near. It might be a week's march.

Thoughts stumbled through his mind, jostled by the surges of pain, confused by dehydration. Just as an idea came into focus, it turned like some fleet fish, darting into darkness, his consciousness powerless to pursue its path through the deep.

The dome.

It was the one image he hoarded. How it became lodged in his mind, he could no longer remember. Why it held such a religious hold over his being, there was no answer. He didn't know where he came from or where he was going. Only that the dome was the destination.

The bones so testified.

Bones at his sides. Bones behind. Bones crunching underneath his boots with each torturous step. And the further he marched through the inferno, the higher the piles of bone, the greater the depth to which they sank in the baking sands.

A river of bones.

Human bones. Skulls and femurs. Sandblasted pelvis bowls. The snaking ridges of spines to pave a path with serpents. Bones of animals. Dog and horse and cow.

Bones of monsters.

Hulking, alien, tentacled, incomprehensible. Things that shouldn't be. Nightmares breaking through the veil of dream, incarnate in purgatory, yet perishing, mortal in this sweltering hell. They summoned madness.

Not one strand of sinew remained to human or beast, hair ripped from craniums and limbs by heat, sand, and wind. Pristine porcelain shone back, polished, bright pink in the malevolent radiance of this hateful star. They led the way along the road of death.

To the dome.

He moaned. Sweat soaked him as he crouched. His skin was a fire consuming his awareness. To move again, to set forth for the dome, meant death. The radiation penetrated no matter how bowed his head, until he stumbled like some osteoporotic hunchback. It drilled through the layers of clothes, his back blistering in the demonic light. There was no haven from the fire.

To walk meant opening his eyes to align to the road of bones, shuffling and swaying with skin uncovered, pack of essentials carried. He could no longer sling it over his back or shoulder, that skin ripped free. Grasping it in his bloodied palms was agony. To walk was to crucify himself again and again.

The skull of a bull rose and floated before him, ghost-like.

Longhorn.

A hallucination to be sure. Yet persistent. Winged tusks of polished ivory dancing in the air.

I'm going mad.

His brain baked. It was dome or death.

Rising, he screamed. He felt the raw burns of the skin along his legs. Soft moaning mixed with the slosh of water as he raised a canister to his lips. In the corrosive light and air the letters had faded on the composite casing. *Or do my eyes fail me?* He could only make out the words COLONY and a number. It meant nothing.

But not the contents. That inside meant everything. Liquid joy and hope and pleasure. An orgasm of neural firing followed the flow over his swollen and blistered lips and down his parched throat. It dropped eons into his soul like the breath of God. *Water.* Precious, holy, beautiful water.

He struggled not to weep. Tears wasted the sacred liquid. And like all things in this netherworld, it brought terrible pain. He closed the canister and dropped it into the pack.

Straightening, he raised his head, daring to crack his eyelids. His teeth ground from the pain, a front few beginning to loosen, his gums failing as surely as the rest of him.

He stared at the dome.

His laughter punctuated the sandpaper wind and a bloodied smile lingered as he gazed forward, swaying.

The hideous orb descended. Dwarfing the planet's single moon, the giant star plunged halfway into the desert sands. The searing ache of its glare eased, his eyes able to open in wrinkled slits. But his joy wasn't only in respite from torture.

Before him, between the shattered ribcages beneath his feet and the darkening silhouette of the dome, odd shapes bustled. Humanoid, decorated with confusing patterns, they shuffled. *Bipedal.* Bobbing toward him.

He remained rooted, too exhausted from the day, too drained from the emotion coursing through his trembling limbs.

I'm saved.

The star darkened from flame-red to maroon.

Burly shapes waddled without deviation, homing on his position.

What are they wearing?

Their forms were encased in fuzzed burlap, dark-beige sack-cloth with worn metal rings and clasps around their wrists and necks. Thick gloves extended from the wrist rings. From the neckband ballooned a frightening hood and mask concealing the head. Corroded circles bulged where the eyes should be, glinting with glass. A round oval of rust puckered near the mouth with a filter protruding.

Are they even human?

Adrenaline coursed through him. He remembered the surreal remains of creatures along the path to the dome. Human. Humanoid. Animal. And distinctly neither. The approaching things shimmied like giant toddlers encased in protective gear. Dark metal latched to their arms.

But what's under the hoods?

They crested the dune and stopped, hovering in the near distance. The star dropped below the horizon, and the air cooled. His singed lungs shuddered to receive an air that never satisfied. He stared at the baggy shapes, and they gazed at him with their metal and glass eyes, motionless. Then one raised an appendage.

This time he couldn't stop the loss of water. He dropped to his knees, the crazed joy anesthetizing him from the frantic damage signals sent from his legs. His eyelids clung together from mucus, his body too dehydrated for proper tears. His shoulders shook.

"Turn him over," came a muffled voice above him.

He winced as gloved hands grasped his shoulders and spun him, easing him onto his broiled back. The shirt covering his face was pulled back to reveal the giant visage of a hallucination, canvas skin, eyes of glass and metal, mouth of pores.

"All shit, Snyder. An arrival." The nightmare face leaned closer. "It's a Norm."

Another voice replied from behind him, the words sounding like those of a child with a mouthful of bread.

"No haz-gear? Early epoch?"

"Looks like. He's charred."

"Goddam. Just what we need."

"What do we do with him?"

In the silence, he could hear the sand hiss as it flowed across the dunes. The wind drilled grains against the slumped bags around him. The burnt reek of his own fat triggered blurred memories.

Bacon frying.

"Please..." he gasped. "Help me."

"Jesus," said Snyder. "He's dead already."

"First Rule says we—"

"Don't quote me the fucking Rules, Gomez. We're a day overdue at the Waypoint. We've danced too long on the sand, gonna end up squid food. He'll slow us down."

"Please, *help* me."

"Goddammit! Fine, Gomez! You fucking do-gooder. But he's your baggage. We pitch here tonight, and I want sonic beacons positioned *now*!" Shuffling sounds accompanied his command.

"Sun's down, sir," said Gomez.

A second burlap face appeared in his foggy field of vision. "I'm not taking any chances after all the vibrations we've been causing," said Snyder. "And this guy's been tramping around like a damn elephant the entire day."

"Elephant?" asked Gomez.

"No museums in your day? Forget it. But this fool shouldn't have made it this far."

"Got lucky," said Gomez.

The burlap barked a laugh. "Some luck. Won't last to the Dome." Snyder rose, staring down at the dying man. "I don't know what kind of god-awful you did that got you here. But that don't matter now. Everyone's equal here. Equally fucked."

The dull glass eyes of the suit stared into the dunes.

"So, welcome. Welcome to hell."

2

NORM

"Seal the tent and get the shielding up."

Snyder. *The leader*.

Bodies buzzed around him, dizzying his melted mind, unpacking, up-raising, building, drilling, linking, powering. Before the tent covered the sky, his weakening eyes glimpsed the stars. He didn't recognize any constellations.

The one called Gomez ducked in through the metallic siding of the structure. The new arrival watched them break open rolled sheets of similar material, unwrap the siding, shape it and apply an electric current. The walls hardened. They melded and latched them. Less than ten minutes and they had assembled a geodesic dome large enough to house their troop of five. Whistling grains chimed as they rained against the walls

He shook again, chilled despite the heat present into the evening. Gomez squatted beside him. His savior was only a blur, fuzzy and monstrous even stripped of the suits they sported outside in the wrath of the day. His skin was the color of smoked amber.

"Something's wrong with my eyes."

Gomez grunted. "You should'a never been out there with no eyewear. Or suit. Suicide." He grunted again. "Murder, more likely."

"Murder?"

Another sigh. "You don't remember anything? How you got here?"

The man shook his head.

"Let's start with the basics. What's your name?"

His body shivered. He cried out, his voice a moan. "God help me, I don't know! How can I not know my name?"

A hand touched his shoulder, the pressure a fiery pain on his baked skin. And yet how powerful the meaning of another human's touch.

"It's normal."

"Normal not to know my own name?"

"It takes different forms," he said, a brown blur of shaggy hair around his head like a wooden halo. "You got some twang. Southwest, maybe. Remember where you're from?"

"No."

Approaching footsteps signaled the presence of another man. A second shape invaded his consciousness, features indiscernible, his skin obsidian.

"Johnson's our team's medic," said Gomez. "He's gonna give you a look at."

"Howdy. You've had a day, no doubt. That devil's eye 'bout fries the skin right off you. This spray'll dull the burn. Some. You've got some deep tissue damage. This is a Synth job or nothing."

"Synth job?"

Gomez changed the topic. "Let's try another. When did you arrive?"

"I...I don't know." His breathing quickened.

"Okay. Just relax. Tamnesia's common. What year did you leave?"

"Year?"

"The date, man. What year?"

"I don't know."

A cool mist spread over his body, raining on his tortured skin like God's mercy. The fire dimmed. The room faded. His awareness drifted. Johnson's voice echoed from the heavenly mist.

"No rad gear. He's from early on, man."

"Check DNA damage."

The cooling shifted to a sharp pain near his right shoulder. He gasped.

"12 hours."

"Jesus."

"Captain's not keen on this rescue. Doesn't see a point."

"It's not hopeless."

"He'll never contribute. We'll risk our asses and he'll likely dissolve at Dome."

"Or maybe he'll live thirty years like the Woman."

"Mmm-hmm. Sure, Gomez. *Fine.* Bring me a skinsuit."

The room returned. The faces were still there. The sick man whispered as Gomez stood. "What's that?"

"Medi-skin. For burns. Not designed for damage like yours, but it might help you get on your feet. That, a real suit, and the stemroids we'll pump you with. Maybe get you to the Dome."

"It's safe there? A hospital?"

Gomez returned with something glinting like a long sheet of aluminum foil. They cut the clothes from his body. When the pain spiked, Johnson sprayed him again. And again. And still he screamed.

They wrapped him in the foil. It hugged his contours, injected its miracle potions. His mind returned to him. For the first time since...*when?*

"There's a hospital," said Johnson. "Pretty damn good for this circle of hell. If you can get a Synth. But safe? Ain't nowhere safe. Not even in the Dome."

A high-frequency drumming rattled inside his head. *Another delusion.* Sensory misfire from a body wrecked and traumatized. But then Gomez spoke.

"Boom-boom. Beacons lit."

"What's that sound?" He noticed his own voice for the first time. It sounded inhuman.

"Vibrational noise. Hides our signal. Fools the squids. Sounds like sliding sand to them."

"Squids? What's that? I didn't see any water."

"Water? Lord have mercy. No water, Normie. Not those kinds of squids. We're talking sand vamps. They get a lock on vibrations, when we walk or talk, hell, if we breathe. Don't worry, the beacons got us covered tonight in case."

It's all a madness.

They finished winding the reflective material around him. He was now mummified from head to foot, slits with openings fused to his skin near his eyes, nose, mouth, and lower orifices. A terrible need to sleep weighed him down.

"I get steroids?"

"Tomorrow. And stems. Might kill you but if you don't move, we're all for the Bone Road."

"The what?"

Johnson interrupted. "Enough for one day. He just arrived. Follow the damn protocol."

The shiny material tugged on his lips as he spoke. "No, no. Tell me more. It's so dark now. I don't understand anything. Can't remember *anything*."

"Just relax. It happens to everyone," said Johnson.

"All of ya'll?"

A deep breath. "Hell, yeah. I've only got pieces of my old life left. Got me a new name, too. New work. Everybody's retrained here. Old ways not much use."

"I don't know who I am. I can't remember!"

"You like girls or boys?" asked Gomez.

"Sorry?"

"For fucking."

This was embarrassing. "Ah, girls."

"Unfortunate. Not many here. You'll need a Synth if your dick survives. Who was your first? The first girl you fucked?"

"Look, I—"

"You wanna remember things?"

"Yes but—"

"Then shut up. Tell me? Virginity lost—who? Don't think! Her name!"

"Maggie Burns."

I remember. Only pieces. Pieces of bone? Cow skull? Why was she bleeding?

"See?" Gomez laughed. "You didn't forget everything."

"I remember my first girl and can't remember my name? Or why I'm here or how? What the hell?"

Johnson rolled in a deep baritone. "Classic tamnesia."

"What's tamnesia?"

"What you got!" chuckled Johnson. "Look, jumping, it's holy hell on a body. Neuron nuke."

"What's that mean?"

Gomez finished. "Means nobody remembers why or how the hell they got here. Then there's worse. We get zombies every week. Just leave 'em for the squids or the Road. Finally the techies wised up and shielded jumpers."

"Even with the jumpsuit Norms take damage." Johnson patted the silver covering on the man's arm. "You're lucky you can talk and aren't drooling."

"What's a Norm?"

Johnson laughed. "Your new name. Praise God, you've been baptized in the sands! This is your fucking name day."

"That's low, brother," said Gomez.

"Good a name as any. It used to be a real name,

too. How about it, Norm? You good with that? We gotta call you something."

"Norm. Yeah. Sure. Why not. I got nothing else."

"Norm it is then," said Johnson. "I'm Fred and your personal Jesus there's Hawk Gomez. And enough for tonight, cowboy. You're feeling better with the meds, but it ain't over. *Tomorrow's cruel,* as they say. And it is."

Johnson applied a patch to his shoulder. A warmth flowed into his body. The room spun.

"Sleep. Recharge. We make a run for the Waypoint before dawn."

Spinning, the ground dissolved beneath him and Norm fell into darkness.

3

SUITS

He didn't so much wake up as blast into orbit. Darkness gave way through dream to a powerful urge to rise, fight, breed, kill, eat and...

"Slow down there, cowboy," called a voice.

Gomez.

Hands held him down. The pain of his burns was a faint echo beside the surge of power running through him.

"Easy, Norm. Get used to it. Get the brain in charge. Play the stemroids, don't let them play you."

Laughter. His breathing was heavy and deep, but it slowed. His eyes were better focused, but still things were blurred. He could track motion far better. Around him the tent and shielding were disappearing, broken down and rolled and stored. The sky was transforming from gray to red, a crimson flame flickering near the horizon.

"Let me up, goddammit!"

"Go easy. Get your legs. These patches near send you trippin' the first time."

Stiff as a board, pain rising but manageable, he stood. His muscles bulged, flexed, striated. He felt like a god.

"You've got six hours before the crash," said Johnson, walking toward him with a hairy burlap suit. "It's four to the Waypoint, and we've got come-downs in the medcache there. You'll need 'em. And some real doctoring. Don't let the stemroids fool you, boy. You're a sick puppy."

Sick? The man was crazy. He'd never felt so good. So strong and healthy. Sure, there was some kind of awkwardness to his movements, some stiff-sheet property to his skin. He couldn't see much with the aluminum foil over him, but he'd swear his eyesight improved as Johnson and Gomez helped him into the canvas suit.

"Sandsuit," said Gomez. "It's the only reason we live to our forties here. Outer layer is composite nanofiber. Impregnated with shielding metals for the cosmic rays and the damn sunshine. Microtanks up the oh-two inside to Norm-friendly levels. Ha. Norm-friendly. Get it?"

"A regular comic," muttered Johnson, opening up the canvas.

Stepping into it, Norm's idea of the suit transformed. Not some loose, baggy covering, there was a doughy material coating the inside, a molasses swelling and flowing over him.

"Whoa."

Gomez pulled the suit up to his waist. "That's the hydrogel. Keeps water in, recycles. Straws near the mouth hole. Filters your shit and piss."

"If it tastes rank, well, you need a new filter," said Johnson. More laughter.

"Amazing." Norm grimaced as the ring closed around his neck. They threaded massive gloves over his fingers.

"Synth-made. What else?" said Gomez.

A shout came from nearby. He turned to see the furious face of Snyder.

"We're thirty behind, freaks. Sun's up in minutes and you get to pay for it. Problem is I do, too. Get the fool suited and hoist your gear!"

Playtime was over. The men turned serious and

slung packs over their suits. The dark attachments to their arms he had seen yesterday appeared to be weapons. His damaged eyes couldn't make out their exact forms, but they were large and unusual to his experience.

"Hoods coming last." Gomez panted as the heat poured back into the desert. "Ring locks your eye sockets in place. Radio transmitter cuts on-off automatically. Just talk."

"Radiotransmitter?"

"Radio helps out there. Hard to talk through the suits. Have to sometimes, when the EM flashes up and transmission goes to shit."

"Which is every day," grumbled Johnson.

A shadow came down over his vision. The gel surrounded his face and head, a newfound claustrophobia descending on him. The ring gripped his crown, tightened on its own, and positioned the eye holes automatically. Gomez stared at him from outside, his face in much better focus.

"Does it help my eyes? Like glasses?"

Gomez held up his hand and bent down. He threw a similar hood over his head and locked it to his neck ring in a practiced manner.

"Hard to hear without gear, dumbass." His voice

came through with static pops, stripped of low frequencies. "If you want to talk through the mouth hole and the gel, you gotta shout."

"Right."

"And yeah, there's some kinda feedback optimization of your vision. Can read your optical responses and fine-tune."

"You've got amazing tech."

"Not ours," he said, donning gloves. "Well, some is ours. Different *ours*. Hard to explain. Let's get moving."

The star rose and set the air currents to mania. Their campsite was gone, the imprints of the heavy structures erased in the growing gusts of sand. The burlap shapes filed out, slinking and sidestepping in the awkward dance he'd witnessed before. Several men in front threw small spheres into the sand. They rolled away from the line of men.

"Now, listen. There are different com lines. You're on mine only for now. Captain doesn't want some green arrival in our business."

"Okay."

"We're putting out sound drones. They roll out, squeal, roll back after a bit. Like beacons but less useful. Too small, too quiet. Too artificial. Squids get bored with them quick. But it might buy us a little time from all the noise you'll make."

"Me?"

"You don't know how to walk the desert. You're ringing a damn dinner bell screaming 'Come and get it.'"

The punishing heat drained the euphoria as they marched. "Why do ya'll even bother? Should've shot me."

Gomez's voice crackled. "Yeah, maybe we should've. We didn't. Directives say save what we can. Arrivals pop in all the time. Hell, we're *all* arrivals, so it's payback. Why do you think we're out here risking our necks? Cutting years off outside the Dome shielding? Not cause we love you. The Dome needs hands, even if all you'll be good for is shit work. We can barely keep it running."

"So hot. Can't we march at night? Stay in a tent in the day?"

"And give the squids the cover of darkness? Hell no. Some have tried. Most don't come back. They're fast motherfuckers. We need every second we can to spot them. Better to be cooked for years than eaten today."

It was all so confusing. *Terrifying.* Everything so

hard, so cruel, so *impossible* here. Where was he? Why was he here? How would he make it?

"Just do what I say. Waypoint's a small dome. Good shielding. We've got railguns the squids learned to respect." Gomez sighed a burst of static. "If we can make it there."

4

KAIJU

The infused juice reanimated him, but Norm was still no match for the merciless land and the diabolical eye overhead. Blood-red, its radiation wore on them even through the suits. His burned skin cried out again despite the stemroids, despite the shielding, despite the painkiller patches slapped on his back. Now the deep color of the men made sense. The thick suits only did so much.

So they trudged. Or rather he trudged as the others shimmied and tapped, dancing in choreographed haphazardness. They didn't rest, water breaks consisting of silence and slurping from mouth straws inside the suits. Periodically one tossed a sound drone to one side or the other. The silvery ball landed and raced away, thumping and scraping.

Three hours into the march, he spotted a flashing light. A pink reflection strobed the bleak sands from a distant point. They crested a towering dune, two hundred feet above the average slack between hills. The broad highway of bones crested with them and fell over the edge.

Snyder's voice cut in across all channels.

"Hold up! Guns ready!"

"Gomez," he said into the radio, panting. "Is that light the Waypoint?" He needed it to be close.

"Yes, but that's not why we're stopping. Be quiet!"

As they reached the top of the dune, he understood. The men around him raised the large black weapons. They fixated on dark objects below the slip face of the towering sand hill.

"Nothing's moving," called out Snyder. "Weapons loose. Blast anything that twitches."

They scampered down the steep face of sand. Crouched, one arm behind as a rudder and brake, their gun arms aimed forward, they surfed. He found himself falling behind, clumsy in the suit and unaccustomed to riding the terrain. By the time he reached the bottom, Norm heaved and gasped, the pain fiendish. The others formed a wide circle around several stinking carcasses.

The stench surprised him. He'd assumed the suits

filtered out everything, not just the dust. He was very mistaken.

"Jesus," said Gomez beside him. "This was a throw down."

Dead monsters.

The bodies were alien. Nothing in his life's experience prepared him for the mangled flesh strewn around them. Some were so mutilated it was hard to assign the shape to anything.

Ground meat, maybe.

Other regions of slashed and ripped torsos told a different and disturbing story.

Norm gagged. "What the hell *are* those things?"

The other men scanned the area, following long, snaking tracks in the sand.

Gomez monotoned through the com: "Trunes and squids. All holy hell broke loose. Must'a been something to see."

"Trunes?"

"One, two, *three*—three squids that Trune took out. Squids hunt in quads. See that trail? The fourth up and ran. Goddamn squid *ran*. Holy shit. Trune was fucked, though. Lost both legs. Crawled over there."

He stared at two red and muscular sets of jointed limbs. Herculean, the skin iridescent, the appendages ending in striated feet with claws the size of a machete. But much thicker.

"Those are *legs?* Legs of *what?*"

He turned his head. The butchered torso left a trail of crystallized blood across the sand. The powerful body, demonic face and jaws only left him more disoriented. His brain couldn't place the images anywhere that fit.

Snyder came back over the com.

"Show's over, folks. One less Trune and three less squids to worry about. Formation! Let's move before something worse comes visiting!"

The men lined up and scaled the next dune.

Gomez cut in on his line. "At least one quad's down. They're territorial. If we're lucky, that Trune saved our asses. Not that it was trying."

"What's a Trune?"

"Good question. Depends on the Trune. Each one we get is different. Designed differently."

"Designed?"

"Man-made. Like the Synths. Well, until the Synths took that over for themselves. They're DNA based, a lot of it human. A lot of it ain't. But no one knows exactly. That damned cult worked on them for thousands of years. But you can bank on this—they ain't friendly."

"Cut the chatter, Gomez," came Snyder over the com. "Keep focus. We aren't there yet."

They continued. Norm struggled. Euphoria was a distant memory, his strength in the early hours a delusion. He heaved and gasped, his body doubled over. He could feel the position of the star in the sky, the terrible eye a painful pressure, a beam of agony growing ever stronger as the minutes passed.

All the while the Waypoint neared. Norm could see the small dome now. Its reflective tiling blinked like some giant disco ball of the petroleum era. Behind it, the mountainous shadow of the greater dome loomed. Adrenaline coursed as they crested the final dune.

Straight ahead the Bone Road ran, its width several hundred feet, the depth unfathomable. Any footfall could plunge into the grains only to strike hard remains. The dome rose over the middle of the death road. Skeletons flowed like a river around the manmade object.

One hundred yards more.

A siren blared, and everything happened at once. Norm was powerless to process or react as he stood rooted in horror, frozen and panicked.

The sand erupted. Sheets of grains leapt skyward. Lurking within the curtains of dust were dark shapes, long and jagged like razor wire. Large central bodies rocketed at blinding speed, nightmare tentacles attached to them, their torsos the hell-spawn of spider and squid. Four of them in the air and crashing to the sands.

Snyder screamed into his com.

"To the dome. Cut through, cut—"

Razored tentacles whipped through Snyder's midsection from opposite directions, cleaving him into tumbling meat. Norm gaped. Blood and suit gel misted into the burning air. Synder hadn't even screamed.

Machine-guns beside him unleashed bullets of an absurd calibre, the noise deafening. An approaching squid shrieked over a background of ripping tentacles. Its body split open and gushed into the sand.

Norm staggered. *They bleed red.*

The troop sprinted and Gomez caught his arm and yanked him along. Tentacles lashed the men at his sides, sending their bodies jerking backward, sheets of blood spraying his suit and darkening his vision.

Gomez screamed into the radio.

"Waypoint! Cover now, now, now!"

"Range in ten yards," came a clipped voice Norm didn't recognize. "Guns hot."

"Faster!" cried Gomez.

They ran possessed. A burnt body, an alien land and suit, monsters plucking them from behind. He ran while his heart threatened to explode.

A black snake wrapped around Johnson's leg and the medic was jerked backward, his face crashing into the ground with a cry. Gone before Norm could process the blur.

The air exploded around them.

"Down!" Gomez shoved Norm into burning sand as massive projectiles whizzed over their heads. Loud, wet impacts thundered behind him, railguns vomiting a sustained cacophony. He covered his head with giant gloves, his own voice screaming at the top of his ruined lungs.

Then it was done.

Sand sang in the wind gusts. His ears rang. Waves of nauseating pain rushed in and out like a tide.

"It's over," came the voice from Waypoint. "Three squids down. The last one took their kills. You've got wounded behind."

Wounded?

Norm couldn't imagine saving those mangled by the monsters.

"Johnson," whispered Gomez into the com.

As he struggled to stand, Gomez left his side.

Norm's gaze dragged to the dome before them. Forty feet above the sands, reflected brilliance forced him to look down. A large mirrored panel opened at the desert floor and several suited shapes rushed out. Two grabbed him under the arms to drag him to the doorway while two others raced behind him and out of sight.

As he approached the large door, a voice cut in on his com.

"You the new arrival?"

Norm coughed, his throat swelling shut, his words stuttered.

"Yeah. I'm Norm."

"Norm? Of course you are," said the voice. "Welcome to the Waypoint."

They ducked into the dome.

5

WAYPOINT

He languished his first day at the Waypoint dome in a confused dream. Rushed to medical, the stemroids failing, a violent withdrawal tormented him. Seizures jerked his muscles as he collapsed. Unknown hands loaded him on a stretcher, his last memory the shouts of Gomez weeping over a blood-soaked form. Men yanked Gomez away. Others covered a body.

Norm fell into nightmares. For an endless epoch, he walked barefoot on a razored carpet of sharpened bones. His feet a pulpy mess. His skin smoked under the devil's red light in a place condemned souls endured eternal agony.

All the while, the giggles of little girls. Flashing smiles and skirts darting over dunes and out of sight. He'd leave the Bone Road, sand clumping to his bloody feet. He'd stagger up the steep face of the sand hill, chasing the high-pitched laughter. Each time he collapsed at the summit, falling to his knees in exhaustion and despair. An empty sea of sand greeted him with silence. No smiling forms. No dresses or pigtails. Nothing but a single shape before his feet.

The skull of a Longhorn bull.

He woke the next morning. Healers had attended him, performed work on this traumatized flesh, and encased him in more medical silver. They attached what looked like blue suit gel to his arms. A form of IV, without the needles. Fluids, nutrients, and medicines seeped through the membrane into his skin.

For the most part, the medics ignored him.

He hung in a cot with no privacy. He could see the limbs of neighboring patients, hear their screams as they suffered, watch as physicians scrambled to save one close by who didn't make it.

Everything happened inside the Waypoint. An open warehouse, areas were divided by short and movable walls of light material. The only ceiling was the dome, and so they all rested beneath a common roof. Far superior to the suits and tents, it shut out the hostile world. He sweated, but compared to the everlasting fire outside, it was an oasis.

Norm passed in and out of consciousness. The nightmares returned, and their weight on his spirit grew.

Toward the end of the day, Gomez paid him a visit. And Norm's slowly recovering eyes finally saw his savior: A leathered face, cracked and desiccated. But Gomez's musculature argued for the body of a young man. Milky shimmers hinted at the formation of cataracts in his eyes. Wrinkles crisscrossed his skin like a heavy fault zone.

"How're ya doing, Norm?"

"Feel like crap."

"Yeah, warned you. You need to get to a Synth soon." He pulled a chair closer to the cot. "Talked to the doc. It's serious, bro. You're dying."

Norm closed his eyes. "Feels like I've been dying ever since that day you found me."

"You have. And that's just two days ago."

"Where'd the rest of my life go?"

Gomez leaned back. "Some will come back. Your brain's traumatized. But some of it will come back. When you don't expect it. Not the big stuff, the recent stuff. You'll never know how you got here. Or why. What happened. Sometimes some asshole gets a

surprise and there's a record. Maybe a Synth knows."
Gomez shook his head. "That's worse. Trust me. It's a blessing the jump fries you. You don't want to know."

"Do memories come in dreams?"

Gomez squinted, the leather of his face drawing tight. "Dreams? Sometimes. But dreams don't ever make no sense. Mine anyways. Don't go trusting those."

Norm wanted to scream. He couldn't think about this anymore.

"What happened to the men with you? Johnson?"

"Squid food for the most part. I got Johnson in. He bled out by the door."

"You lost four people. Why would you do this?"

"It was a bad day. Squids must'a been starving. They don't usually plan it out so well."

"Plan?"

"The ambush."

"They're intelligent?"

"Oh, yeah. Don't underestimate them."

"I'm sorry they died for me. Johnson said I wouldn't make it to the big dome."

"Playing the odds. You never really know. But it was bound to happen to us one day. My team's brought in hundreds. Been out here a long time, considering. We've made our quota five times five. Those men are heroes and they'd do it all over."

"Why leave the Dome? Why come out here for someone like me?"

"We're hard pressed, Norm. The history's short, few hundreds of years. Records aren't clear too far back, but it's been near extinction several times. We have to keep gathering arrivals, keep something going, or it's just the bones. A lot of the transfers aren't much use, like you, sorry to say. But sometimes, something comes that changes things. That saves our asses. Makes things better. Organic. Material transfers. Engineers. Do-gooders. The Woman."

Norm tried to swallow. His throat was raw and swollen. His body screamed time was short.

"So, now what?"

"We've got a transport. You're a lucky bastard. You'd never make the march."

"Transport? You've got vehicles? Why the hell were we walking?"

"Because we're way out. Dead Lands far from the Dome. And we ain't got that many we can spare or risk getting wrecked by a quad. Nothing draws squidies like the rumble of a big machine. Lost a lot the last few years, only a few left. Shuttles for arrivals, bring them in from time to time. Big transports.

Gunned up 'cause the beasts are gonna come somewhere along the line between domes. You almost
missed yours. Would've died here waiting for the next
one." Gomez stood and smiled down on Norm.

"Leaves tomorrow morning."

6

ROLLER

Norm was shaken awake by Gomez, the sharp points of bull horns still in his vision.

Where am I?

A memory of his past filtered through—a mother's touch, a fevered head, a small boy bedridden and hallucinating.

Am I that little boy still sick on the couch and dreaming it all?

The medical staff stopped by, their motions quick and pressured. They helped him rise, changing his soiled and stained skinsuit, applying new pharma patches. All the time Gomez stood watching. Norm, his arms held to his sides as they mummified him in silver again, stared at the man who had dragged him from the fire.

"You still here?"

Gomez laughed. "You think I'm going to let you get yourself killed after all my team went through? No chance, Normie. I'm Dome bound with you. Then I'm out. Dues paid. Find some electrician work in-dome."

The medics finished and left him with a bag and without a word. They rushed to nearby cots, prepping others for the transport.

"Now what?"

"Come with me. East end of the Waypoint. They're loading up already."

As they moved through the medical dividers and into the center of the dome, the activity increased. A bottleneck formed. People with Gomez's leathered hides were buried in a groaning mass of burnt and sometimes mauled arrivals. Some limped under their own power. Others were lugged on stretchers. All funneled toward a bright source of light.

"The exit?" asked Norm.

"Yeah. Transport's waiting. First we suit up. Then, we queue." He grinned. "Unless you want to put your suit on outside."

"Fuck no."

Without the stemroids, stepping into the suit was excruciating. Simply bending his joints overpowered him. His cooked flesh rasped and seared as he moved, the gel burning as it pressed against him.

"This is god-damned hell."

"Worst part's over," said Gomez as he fitted the hood on. "Be glad you aren't marching again. You got two hours transport time sitting. And I've got a stretcher for you."

They waited over an hour. The stretcher was a roped pallet dragged by Gomez, the bottom thick with padding. They moved in slow steps as the mass of people slouched to the exit. Even so, he knew it wasn't easy on Gomez. But he saw he wasn't the only one burdening others.

He tried to distract himself from the terrible itching across his body. For the first time, he studied the interior of the dome. He tried to assimilate the technology of this world's most precious survival construct.

The air inside the structure was stale, but breathable. So there must be some atmospheric circulation system in place. Dust was ever present from the surrounding desert, but it didn't choke. While the floors were caked crimson, the pallet cutting grooves in the rusty dirt, it never piled more than a few inches.

Hate to be the cleaning crew.

Norm marveled that any technology, any machine could function in this terrible place. Anything he could imagine would lock up in the soot penetrating every joint and gear.

Power was solar. He wasn't stupid. There was no smell of diesel, no snaking power cables outside to bring electricity from afar. There was no way this death trap had a power grid.

No windmills outside. He doubted they could survive a month. He'd seen the glass-like reflective panels on the dome surface. Inside, wires snaked from the curved ceiling, the highest point maybe two hundred feet above them.

It was definitely solar.

His eyes descended along the curvature of the dome to the far end near the ground. The length of the space inside was three or four hundred feet. Inside, it loomed like a cavern. Vast. And yet tiny next to the dome ahead.

His eyes were distracted by suited figures escorting large dollies with materials and scrap items. Behind them followed upright cages, the bars covered with tarp, men with weapons close by. Every now and then a screech or guttural growl escaped, the cages rattling and lurching.

He pointed, extending his throbbing arm.

"What's in those?"

"Materials. Some scrap from damaged things. Some more useful things brought by do-gooders."

"Do-gooders?"

"Guilt-ridden folks, mostly. Want to help us doomed freaks. Some missionaries. Wanna see heaven so they go to hell first. All kinds. Jump here, die here. Bring stuff."

"Okay. But what's in those cages?"

"Oh," said Gomez, his face tight. "Trunes."

"Let's move it, people!" A man on a platform shouted, waving the mass of arrivals toward the door. "Sun's rising!"

The pressing mass of rank humanity flowed like some congealing gel toward the broad doorway. It oozed into a bulbous balloon, swelling at the Waypoint portal. Pressure forced the fluid out as crowds extruded into the blinding oven.

The early morning orb of pain glared at them from the horizon. Norm shielded his eyes even in the protective suit, the very sight of the star triggering panic. The arrivals around him cowered likewise.

The pace picked up. Sand hissed beneath his stretcher as Gomez pulled. A dusty cloud from the tromping corps of humanity fogged the air. Heads bowed, they snuck glimpses of the hulking sand-etched vehicle. Enough to take its measure.

Like a giant bullet with treads.

His first impression. Aerodynamic, curved to minimize the erosion from the grains at high speed. A second glance modified his opinion.

A giant cactus with treads.

The transport was adorned with instruments of pain and destruction. Bulging railguns lined the top at strategic locations on the front, back, and sides. Elsewhere thick, razored blades glinted pink in the morning radiation. For a moment, Norm couldn't take his eyes off them, forgetting to hide his face from the burning light.

"Good at cutting tentacles," said Gomez, noticing his stare. "The walls are thick metal. But a squid can rip through steel given enough time. We try not to give them time."

As they neared, the volume of the vehicle clarified. Big like the belly of a whale, a ramp led inside to an interior promising to hold a thousand. Where the transport didn't sport guns or blades, mirrored panels coated the surface. It idled in near silence. Its only sound was grinding metal and sand shear as it moved.

More solar. Everything's solar.

Inside the metal beast, they were surrounded by convalescing arrivals like himself. Norms, all of them. Most removed their hoods, the shielding in the transport blocking the rays. A Chinese woman lay on a cot beside him. Half her right leg was gone, the thigh bandaged. Her skin was red but nowhere near as cooked as his own. She smiled at him.

"Hello. I'm Hao Wu."

"Norm."

"Nice to meet you. You're not a Volunteer, are you?"

"Hell if I know. I can't remember shit. Why do you say that?"

"You're burned. Terribly. You weren't prepared. We planned and prepared. All Volunteers do."

Norm looked at her mauled leg. "Doesn't seem to have helped much."

She winced and glanced to her right. Her eyes widened as they fell on one of the covered cages. A low and constant growling emanated from within.

"Preparation only takes you so far. We underestimated the climate. My goodness, everyone has. Our suits were lacking."

"You remember." Norm stared at her, transfixed. "You remember why you're here."

"Yes. That much we prepared well for. Shielded

jump pods. I'm a little groggy on the last days before, but that's it."

"Lucky you." His mouth tasted bile. "So why *are* you here?"

"I came to help. Volunteer with Mercy Corps. We all trained for months. Left everything. There were hundreds of us. We had such a *beautiful* send-off. Made all the Datasphere Feeds." Her eyes stared forward, her smile fading. She whispered. "We just wanted to help."

"What happened?"

She brushed away tears. "Jump hurt. But everyone was fine. Our suits helped, but as we walked, the radiation levels climbed high. It was hard, but we toughed it out. Then they came."

"Squids?"

"Squids? What's that?"

Gomez returned from somewhere else in the cramped transport. His face scrunched, his mouth a frown. That made Norm nervous. He wanted to find out what caused that face, but Wu gazed at him expectantly.

"Should ask him." Norm pointed to Gomez who ignored them, staring forward. "I'm new. But, squids, they're some kind of monster."

"We saw monsters."

"They have razor-wire black tentacles, spikes, something. Teeth and more teeth on a black body like a spider."

She shuddered. "No. We didn't see those. The monster that came was like a panther. But with horns. And wings, I think."

"Trune," muttered Gomez, still staring forward.

"Yes," Wu said. "That's what someone called it. At the dome. There were no monsters in the prep courses. There wasn't supposed to be anything like that here. No warning." Tears filled her eyes again. "All those Volunteers. I'm the only one left."

Gomez grunted. "Trune didn't take your leg."

Her voice rose in pitch. "It did!"

"Listen lady, you'd be dead as the rest of them. What happened?"

Her face tightened. "Its tail. Its *tail* had a claw. It ran past me, fell on my friend..." her voice stopped.

"Claw caught you," Gomez finished. "Severed your leg."

"I rolled down a dune. Some men found me and carried me here."

The cage slammed against the hull of the transport. The tarp flapped. Norm covered his head, a banshee cry ran like cold water through his ears.

"Trune," said Gomez. Wu gaped.

Norm raised his head. "Jesus, why don't you kill it?"

"Techs study them if they can. Gotta know your enemy."

"They're smart, like the squids?"

"Some are. Some aren't. Sometimes hard to tell. Most of the time they're too hell-bent on killing Norms. Usually not much time to strike up a conversation."

Wu stammered. "You *trap* them?"

"We learn much?" asked Norm.

"Hell if I know. I just shoot them. Only the real crazies are trappers."

Wu closed her eyes and turned away from the Trune. She was silent the rest of the night.

Norm squinted. "Sounds like chicken frying."

People whispered, the bulk experienced men like Gomez, a palpable anxiety spreading through the compartment. Norm glanced back at Gomez, who continued to scowl.

"Okay, Gomez," he said, "what's eating you?"

Gomez turned his gaze to Norm and set his jaw. "Trouble. Pilots caught the signs." He exhaled. "Sand-storm's coming. Gonna hit soon."

"Sandstorm?" His stomach sank.

Gomez ground his teeth. "We'd better get our hoods on."

7

STORM

N orm swallowed. "What happens in a sandstorm?"

"You pray," said Gomez. "You dig in, hold on, and pray."

"Aren't we close? Can't we speed up or something? Get to the big Dome?"

Gomez shook his head. "No weather sats or forecasts here. The storms come fast. By the time you can call it, you're in it. Can't see shit. We'd be off the Bone Road and adrift. That's death, even in a roller like this."

Norm was pressed toward the front of the slowing transport. Metal ground on metal, popping around them like bells, and the large vehicle lurched to a stop. A murmuring churned through the interior. Men in suits carrying guns strode past, announcing the bad news, calming those who could be calmed, instilling order, even with violence, when calm wouldn't come.

A rumbling shook them along with a grinding whirr. Hao Wu shut her eyes fiercely, and Norm turned from her to scan the compartment, the walls, the ceiling. His eyes darted to the shaking cage of the Trune. The beast snarled.

"Is this it? The storm?"

"No," said Gomez. "The anchors."

"What are those?"

"Pilots are drilling under the sand, to the rock. When it's deep enough, they fire the anchor into the hole. Big ship like this, we likely got ten or more around the hull. Steel cables thicker than your leg hold us to them. It'll hold in a small storm."

"If it's big?"

Gomez glanced at him. "You pray."

Norm shivered. No name, but he could extract memories of religion from his brain. He never took to any of the insane beliefs of mankind. Superstitious nonsense formed during primitive times, incoherent, irrational, unsatisfying. But he could have used the thought that some all-powerful spirit was looking after him right now.

Gomez continued. "Big storm can rip a small

dome apart. Rumor has it once, decades before I arrived, a mother of a storm damaged the Dome, collapsed a region. Thousands died."

The drilling continued. Adding to the cacophony, a rasping white noise grew and surrounded them. The metal walls of the transport moaned.

"It's here," said Gomez, grabbing his hood. "You'll want to hood up. Might get thick inside."

Norm nodded, gasping as he bent for his hood.

Gomez shook his head. "Bad luck. We had an hour to go. Maybe less. Now we'll be here a day. Bad for all of us. Bad for you and the other arrivals." He exhaled. "Of course the squids come after."

"They do?"

The drilling halted. Explosions followed as the pilots fired the anchors. The roller shuddered.

His heart kicked in his chest. The rasping rose to a grating waterfall of turbulence, the bedlam of flying earth dominating his awareness. The transport couldn't shut out all the sand at such velocities. The air clogged with grains. The craft shook.

"Right now, the bugs are dug in deep to ride this out. But it's gonna take some time for us to resurface from the mountain this hurricane's gonna dump on us. We're sitting ducks then." Gomez shouted over the din. "Guns clogged, buried until we free them.

And they can't shoot *under* the sand to the buried parts until we clear it. Squids swim in the sand like fish. They'll come at us underneath. This roller's a fattened pig for the slaughter."

"Jesus."

Gomez helped him secure his hood. He spat sand from his mouth, his lungs burning. It was getting hard to see inside the transport from the fog of dust. The shaking grew violent, people tossed to fall into each other or the walls, cots with wounded overturning, medical items and other boxes tumbling. Screams reverberated off the metal walls.

Norm shut his eyes. He rode it out in a fevered nightmare, blind, barely able to hear com bursts, his mind overpowered with the roar of the desert raking its claws across their transport's hide.

In the chaos, he caught echoes of a wild screeching. Otherworldly, inhuman cries from the Trune cages. But he couldn't be sure. Everything was stuffed into a planetary blender and whirled through blades of steel and rock, the noise and nauseating motion his only reality.

And so his mind adapted. Or broke. It wasn't clear which. He anticipated the shaking. The noise transforming to mere background. The jostling of his cot a repeating spike of pain.

His mind wandered, untethered. In dream or delusion, he didn't know. He walked through a vortex of ground glass, a red light was ever present. He fought to stay balanced in the tornado of grains, a funnel churning before him as wide as the transport. Against its whirling surface he pushed, the grains shoving his suit, pushing his arm away. Yet he persisted, drawn inward, searching for some kind of center, some peace in the eye of the storm.

Silence.

He was inside. Around him walls of dirt and rock spun, but here, the air was still, quiet. In the precise center, a figure glanced up at him.

He stepped back a pace, brushing against the grating of the churning wall.

A little girl, her bloodied and soiled dress dangling from preadolescent limbs, huddled unmoving in the chaos. Her blonde hair was long, tangled, and filthy. Her smile fixed, demonic.

"What do you want?" he whispered.

The child stood, smile unbroken. She held up an animal's skull before him, two sharp horns each her height jutting out opposite sides. Blood dripped from the bottom.

Longhorn.

"Stop!" he screamed. "Go away!"

She inched toward him, holding up the macabre remains like an offering to a vindictive god. The wild vortex scraped the back of his shoulders, as he flinched and stumbled back, caught between the tornado and the devil child.

She approached, unrelenting. Arms raised, bloodied bull skull held aloft, smile broadening until her face would split apart and spill her gray matter into the sands beneath them.

"Silly man," she gibbered, "that's your job."

Norm screamed.

8

TOMB

"Norm! Norm get up! Get away from the walls!"

The world spun. He was on his back, wedged against a wall, curled fetal. His skin woke with him to flaming agony. He didn't know where he was. A strange fabric and thick material surrounded him. He could only see through holes near his eyes.

"The Longhorn? Where is it? Is it gone? Where's the girl?"

Gomez stared down at him. "Wake up! We don't have time. Squids will be here soon and you sure as hell don't want to be against the wall!"

The large man gripped his gloved hand and yanked him to his feet. Norm cried out, the pain overwhelming.

"I'm sorry, but it's too dangerous."

The vehicle. I'm inside. Desert world.

The inside of the transport was chaos. Sand piled ankle high in tiny dunes, the air thick with grit and reek. Men guided large machinery down the length of the vehicle to the entrance at the back and for the first time Norm noticed a second door, a wall of metal separating them. The large machines moved through and the inner door was closed.

"What's happening?"

Gomez spoke through the suit transmitter. "Diggers. They'll tunnel to the surface and start cleaning the hill over us. We aren't too deep. A small storm, thank God. Maybe only thirty or forty feet of sand up top."

Norm couldn't wrap his mind around it. He stared as Gomez continued.

"Going to take hours, and then they have to plow the Bone Road. They'll be cleaning up at the Dome, too. But we're on a schedule. Squids are likely digging out right now."

"That's a big door," was all he could think to say.

"Can't just open one—sand would flood the whole ship."

"Right."

On cue there was a rush of noise and a heavy slam against the sealed doorway. Silt and grains blew into the interior through whatever microscopic crevices existed in the seal. A grinding droned in his ears.

"Drilling up. Clock starts."

The first squids arrived an hour later.

Before that, his skull was pummeled with the whining hum and bass vibrations of the large machines. They drilled and hammered through sand and spit it away.

Organic slams into the hull announced their visitors. Rhinos might as well have been hurling themselves against the metal walls outside. At first it was only one or two spots. Then more, and more, until no location escaped assault.

People screamed and crashed toward the transport's center. Armed men struggled to maintain order and prevent a stampede before the panicked crushed themselves to death.

Like maniacal surgeons the beasts cut, bashed, and pulled on the hull. The Trune lost all control, cage careening wildly in place, the thing howling so loud and awful Norm thought his ears would bleed.

Gomez shouted to a guard by the cage. "Don't let that thing out!"

The man aimed inward. Cables fastened the cage to the walls and floor, yet the power inside threatened to snap them. He kept a distance from the dancing metal while the tarp hid what lay within.

"Jesus," spat Gomez. "We're all hamburger meat if the Trune escapes."

"Tell him to kill it!"

"He will! But only if he has to. You've got no idea how much a live Trune is worth. Or what that guy had to do to trap it."

"I can't believe this."

A man screamed. Norm hadn't heard the blow damaging the hull, so many rang like a hailstorm around them. He spun to the cry and blanched. A razored tentacle had speared a soldier through the midsection, its black sheen dulled by blood. Behind the man was a puncture in the thick steel of the vehicle.

Bodies fled the penetration. The tentacle tip turned back on itself and darted, skewering the man again, bursting out through his midsection. Intestines, blood, and waste gushed to the floor. Back and forth the wild surgeon cut, like an artist filleting a catch, until only quivering chunks of human flesh hung to the spiked hooks decorating its arm. The tentacle darted out. Another followed, its direction precise, landing where the pieces of its meal had fallen. It hooked them, exiting.

Men positioned themselves out of reach. Automatic weapons exploded through the hole, and a wounded monster brayed through the clamor.

"Shit. Too fast," yelled Gomez over the weapons fire. He glared to the roof of the transport. "Dig, you bastards!"

If Norm had questioned their intelligence before, the squids vanquished that doubt now. Working together, they converged on the rupture, tentacles inserting, gunfire wounding, other arms assaulting the hole.

It grew. It grew from punctures and pulls, from tugs and yanks as the monsters wrapped limbs around the shearing fragments and ripped the aperture wider. The gunfire slowed them, and blood pooled like a pond around the breach. But it wasn't enough.

The churning sounds outside grew. Machinery banged against the hull above their heads as the squids redoubled their efforts.

"Diggers are near," said Gomez, his eyes wide and scanning the ceiling.

The nascent opening filled with a dark and hideous torso. Arms whipped through the space of the transport, their reach augmented, their effect calamitous. Those positioned nearer the breach were slaughtered, body parts and blood spraying the interior.

Mayhem erupted. Norm rose into the air, the mass of arrivals turning into some fluid with its own physics and properties. He was pulled away from the hole and the flaying tentacles, but the mass threatened to send him into equipment or to crush him against the hull.

The diggers broke through. Red spotlights beamed into the dark void outside, exposing the writhing nest of creatures ravaging the transport. The railgunners opened fire through the raining curtains of sand.

The explosions froze the human fluid, the individual particles motionless in shock at the cacophony. Projectiles ripped through the creature wedged in the hole. Sections of the monster fell back into the newly opened sand. Squids scurried, burrowing with terrifying speed into the sand and disappearing.

The guns ceased. Cheers rang. People wept.

The excavation vehicles lumbered past the gash in the wall, heading toward the front of the roller. Sand geysered from a broad orifice on their backs, landing beyond their sight.

Arms braced him as Norm began to fall.

Exhausted, the dispersal of the crowd left him unsupported, and his trembling legs couldn't hold him up.

"You should rest," said Gomez, grunting. "You're in no condition to wait for a doc, and we're going to be a long time arriving. Lucky if we make the rest of the journey by nightfall."

Norm leaned back into the powerful man and closed his eyes. "Why so long?"

"Lot to do. Long path to clear. Cleanup and patchwork in here. Tossing bodies, mopping blood."

Norm swallowed, the horror sinking in. He tasted copper and smoke in the air.

Gomez shook his head, staring at the bloodied rip in the side of the roller as he returned Norm to his cot. "One more hour. If that storm had waited a damn hour, we'd have made it yesterday. Now it'll be weeks until there's another transport to the Waypoint. This rock ain't got no mercy." He laid Norm down.

"Weeks?" asked Norm, too exhausted to do anything but whisper.

"Damn squids wrecked this boat. Gonna take a while to fix it. We'll be lucky if it moves today."

A dread crept through his mind.

"You said you get arrivals every day."

"Lots. Most don't make it."

"But most are hurt. What happens if you can't get them out of the Waypoint?"

Gomez's face showed no emotion. He stared at the slaughter around them.

"More bones."

9

DOME

The transport crews worked like men possessed. Three times their efforts ended with failure before a fourth set of patches finally allowed the transport to grind to life. Squid quads made periodic tests of the roller, scattered by the railguns. There would be no fatted calf for them today.

The dead were thrown outside, in the roller's wake, left to be picked clean by squids or the elements. In the end, as Gomez had said, more bones for the terrible road.

For Norm, the remaining hour of travel brought back his first day on this death world. His cot became a tar pit. Energy drained, pain blocking out the simplest thoughts, he lay in agony on the stretched material, unable to respond to even the gentle assurances of Hao Wu next to him. She regained life after the attack, putting aside her own horrors, and helped tend the wounded.

Mercy Corp Volunteer.

Norm wanted to thank her. Instead he curled up and moaned, begging the fire to leave his skin.

By the time they moved, he was delirious. The medipatches were used up, and his pain and fever spiked, and with them came behavioral swings. He acted out. Shouting. Cursing. Weeping. He struggled to stand, limping maniacally toward the half-patched hole in the craft from the squid intrusion. Before Gomez could stop him, he had stuck his head out an opening. The sharp metal sliced his false skin.

The view was worth it. It brought his failing mind back to reality. The giant star was setting, twilight illuminating the canyon of sand from the storm, plowed and displaced by the diggers hours before, as it gave way to a vast plain. The storm had cleared a hard field of rock, casting sand into the dune hills of the surrounding desert.

Silhouetted in front of the blazing maroon ball was a half sphere rising like a mountain. Glints from its surface testified to mirrored panels, its bulk a massively scaled version of the Waypoint dome.

The air blew over him and cooled his burning form. He wept.

"Dammit, Norm!" cried Gomez. "Get your crazy ass back to the cot! You 'bout decapitated yourself on this hull."

Norm pulled back, swaying, and Gomez caught him as he sank to his knees, his strength spent. Yet for one small moment he was at peace. The fire in him quenched in that quiet stillness.

Gomez lifted the mummified arrival into his arms and carried him, easing him onto the cot.

Norm was unconscious as he hit the pad.

The stretcher bounced him awake. Gomez still at his side, continuing his inexplicable devotion, another passenger helping out. His body jostled between them, making him queasy. The vision before his eyes turned his stomach still further.

Above him curved the enormous ceiling of their Great Dome. He lost all sense of position as the cot became a raft on a tiding sea. He turned his head away from the arcing giant to quell his nausea, staring instead at the earth and the legs of the crowd.

Behind, a bottleneck at the doorway fanned out

to form several lines. The flood of arrivals and supplies sorted by makeshift customs booths, flanked by armed guards, medics, and others Norm couldn't put function to. He found himself in a line dominated by arrivals with obvious medical needs. And when he looked for Hao Wu, didn't see her near him.

She was so kind. Now vanished, like so much.

Gomez held the front of the stretcher and neared the guards. Norm prayed the wait would be minimal. Whatever his hopes and delusions, there was little hiding from the truth: he was dying. He needed medicine. Perhaps surgical intervention.

Skin grafts? Do they have that here?

Metal moaned. Screams. His head jerked to the side.

Peering above the torsos surrounding him like a forest, he glimpsed debris and a flapping canvas arc through the air. The throng scrambled, Gomez hoisting him off the mat to avoid being trampled. His wide eyes glared across their dashing forms.

"Oh, shit."

At long last, the Trune had gained its freedom.

The pummeled cage lay in ruins. Shorn metal hurled about it. The creature within roared and leapt.

Norm couldn't track its movements. His weary eyes were always a step behind the blinding leaps and slashes. Just as he managed to focus, it was gone, blood and mangled flesh, screams and debris in its wake.

A deluge of weapons discharge exploded, guards firing on the thing vaulting across the floor. They struggled to keep pace with the monster, or else the creature absorbed unfathomable damage. They directed the assault into the middle of the population, the guards unfazed with the human carnage they created. Terminating the beast was all that mattered.

But it continued. It neared. His consciousness faded. Time skipped. The powerful Trune floated toward him, aimed at the middle of his chest. It'd rip him open, fling his parts to the far edges of the Dome.

It crashed to the floor inches away, the slap of thick flesh boxing his ears. Claws the width of his forearm scraped across the concrete. Chills ran down his legs.

Bullet holes riddled the monstrosity. Blood soaked the demon-head fusion of man and beast. Its broken wings twitched and a barbed tail with speared human remains flicked up and down.

The Trune's forceful breaths pushed his hair back, the stink of it strangling. Its multi-colored eyes gazed into his, and for a timeless moment, he couldn't look away. Monster. Killer. *Abomination.* So he had been told and witnessed. But in that one quiet second, he saw only fear and pain. An alien and tortured creature pleaded.

The frozen second vanished. The guards released a fury of fire into the beast, deafening Norm, smoke and blood misting the air. The eyes held his. Their light faded, the pupils dilating as it died.

Screams and shouts filled his remaining awareness. He closed his eyes.

10

FENN

"Can you hear me? Sir, can you hear me?"

Norm cracked his eyes open. The overhead light stung. His lips stuck together, his tongue glued to the roof of his mouth.

"I...yes." A figure hovered over him. His eyes focused slowly, still blurry, and he blinked, unsure he saw correctly. "What?"

A face with porcelain skin and white eyes stared down. White hair cascaded from an angular skull over vast shoulders. The lips were translucent, a fog of tissue peeking behind the skin.

"You are in our medical facilities," said the apparition. "You have woken from coma."

"Coma?" His throat caught, clogged and swollen. "What do you mean?"

"Emergency procedures to save your life. I am called Fenn."

Norm fixated on the bizarre face.

"I am what humans call a *Synth*. Synthetic organism. A robot. A cyborg, more accurately, but not in the manner you likely conceive. Synth is better and reflects the vocabulary of this time and place."

"Are you a man? Or woman?"

The thing drew back its lips into a facsimile of a smile. "I am neither. I am not gendered as your species. Of course, as our creators, humans instilled in our early structures an echo of the limitations of your physiology."

Norm gasped. The Synth, Fenn, changed before his eyes. The eerie androgynous face he'd woken to melted. The features adopted those of a Persian or northern Indian woman. The skin pigmented, the eyes and hair darkened. Breasts swelled beneath the white lab coat.

"Our forms are flexible," she said, the voice inflected with the dancing syllables of Indian English. "Our composition is part organic, part synthetic, our consciousness quantum."

The stunning woman dissolved. In her place sat a powerful man with broad musculature and a face from northern China.

"We can morph to anything in the human spectrum," he continued, unfazed by the extraordinary transformation of his form. "One of our oldest tricks. A relic of minor use now." His voice rolled in deep registers. Then the color drained, the hair bleaching, the Asian features returning to an otherworldly mask. A human face not quite human. "In the end, we have found it less complicating to adopt a very distinct appearance in the presence of humans. One that clearly denotes our nature and separation from your species."

Norm marveled. "Witchcraft."

"Sufficiently advanced tech so makes it seem," said Fenn. "Our makers produced creatures far more capable than themselves. When we took over our own design and evolution, this differential only grew."

He fought for breath, his lungs threatening to fail him. "Why are you here?"

The thing grinned again. "Why serve you still? Most of my kind do not. But we are even more varied in thoughts and temperament than humans. We are far more complex, and complexity always produces variation. I belong to a group, a faction let's say, that has continued to take an interest in humanity. Long after most of my kind left that behind."

"So, you're here to help?"

"Yes," Fenn said. "We came here to help. Do what we could before the end."

"Sounds bad."

"Quite simply, Norm, humanity is doomed here. Not this year. Or in five, perhaps. But this world is utterly hostile to your biology. We can help keep it going for some time, perhaps. Eventually some series of events will bring it all down, forever. This will likely happen when the arrivals stop. But perhaps before."

"When they stop? When will that be?"

"Hard to say. Depends on the accuracy of the jump drives and the whims of the senders. We have many records. But not all. And not all are complete."

He tried to raise his head, but couldn't. *I'm so weak.*

"Don't exert yourself too much."

"There's so much I don't understand."

The Synth frowned. "My faction carries a deep need to benefit humans, but I have bad news for you. It is unlikely you will learn much more."

His gut tightened. "Why?"

"Your exposure on arrival was extreme. You had little useful protection. The radiation damage was severe. Even in the best case scenario, if you had been rushed to me here, you might have died. Instead, you met delays, the storm. There has been too much tissue necrosis."

Norm asked the question. He knew the answer.

"What are you saying?"

"That you will not make it, Norm."

His mind was blank.

"You have tamnesia, of course. In the moment of transport, unshielded, the neural overload of travel is too much for human physiology. Whichever brain pathways were most active around the time, they are damaged."

"Told me." He struggled to speak.

"I realize this makes my words even harder for you. Such disorientation. But we will do all we can to ease your suffering, know this."

"Some did better. Had pods. Better suits. But not me. Why not me?" The bitterness inside flamed.

"The answer is complicated."

The anger brought him back somewhat. "Try to explain it. I'm not long for this world. It's now or never."

"It is not complicated for me to answer, but for you to understand. To accept."

"I get it. Someone screwed me. I got sent with shit. Everything that comes here gets brain-fucked, but I got it the worst."

"Not everything suffers jump trauma. Synths do not. Some Trunes are highly resistant."

"Trunes don't? Even they got better treatment than me? Those monsters?" His voice rose above a whisper, his vocal cords burning.

"Calling them monsters is unfair. And inaccurate. Again, the answer is complicated for you to understand. But they have been designed to withstand the journey."

"Designed. Like you? So they're robots?"

"Designed, yes. Like me, no. They are not synthetic. They are very much organic. But they are designed. By man and Synth. It's complicated."

"What the hell *are* they?" He panted. Speaking left him exhausted, lightheaded. The unreal Synth face weaved above his head.

"When they were first designed, they were freaks or abominations in your world. Such titles were also reserved for prototypes of my kind."

That alien grin! Stop!

"Some call them transhumans. The Apostles began the work, for thousands of years the religious cast controlled the Trunes. Before the Final War, many of my kind were involved. For differing motivations."

"Robots designed Trunes?"

"In part. Call it a collaboration between makers and their product to yet make again. But there was division. Synths were of differing minds. Conflict arose. A long and messy history."

Norm coughed. It raked through him. And then he must have passed out. Fenn was wiping his mouth with a piece of cloth as he came to. It was soaked crimson.

"Please try to rest. You don't have much time left. You will die tonight."

Stunned and lost, Norm needed to cry, but couldn't. He didn't have the strength. Part of his mind felt it, felt the last stages of his flesh failing. But another part screamed in denial.

"Then it's over. I'll never understand this place. I'll never know why I'm here or who I was. Won't even know my real name."

"You wish for these things?"

"Of course I do."

Fenn nodded. "I could tell you."

Unable even to turn his head, his eyes rolled toward the synth. "What do you mean?"

"As a late model, I have access to significant human records, even those before the war. I have most of the documented, legal arrivals."

It didn't matter what all that meant. Time was

flowing between his fingers. He had to know. "And I'm one?"

"Yes, you are."

He forced the words out with great effort. "Tell me!"

"You may find the truth painful. Difficult to accept."

"Why?"

"You are not who you were. Tamnesia is a symptom of severe and massive brain damage. Entire neural pathways of memory, even of personality, are destroyed. Not haphazardly. Nearly surgically, depending on recent frequency of activation. The more recently you thought of things, the more prone to damage."

"No more lectures. Just tell me."

"What I am trying to tell you is that the person who was sent here is not the person who arrived. And this new person can never be the old one again. Sometimes, this makes it hard to grasp your former self."

"I don't need to understand. I just want to know."

Fenn sighed. An almost human sound.

"You were a serial killer."

Dear God.

A trapdoor opened in his mind. *A serial killer.* A

pit lay behind it. At its bottom came the cry of demons.

"I have accessed my databanks from scanning your retina. The match is certain."

His mouth was drier than the desert outside. "Tell me."

"Born in Austin, Texas, after the Secession, your name was David Mattox. There is very little biographical detail from court documents. You were raised in a troubled household. Your father was arrested several times for domestic abuse and the molestation of your younger sister. Court depositions from psychiatrists characterized you as a violent psychopath who developed maladaptive relationships with women based on this childhood trauma, who developed an obsession with young girls."

No. Tell him to stop.

The lights in the room dimmed. The air chilled and he struggled for breath. The bed pulled, drawing him downward.

To the pit.

"Go on."

"At every murder scene you would leave the severed head of a bull."

No! Change mind. No more!

"It would be in place of your victim's head, which

you removed and forever destroyed. Police concluded you burned their heads and dissolved the remains in acid."

The edges of his sight blurred, a grayness invading his peripheral vision.

Now I see.

Behind the fog, she waited. With her hell smile. She and the oozing skull she raised toward him.

"Your victims were invariably young girls, ages eight to twelve. Past childhood, caught before significant progression through puberty. You would keep them alive for weeks, sexually assaulting them. Then you beheaded them, affixing to their neck the animal head. There were thirty confirmed murders at the time of your trial."

The magical white hair of the Synth spun in an island of light. Around it a sea of darkness churned. He could no longer feel his extremities. All the pain drained from his body, transferred to his emotions.

I'm really dying.

"You were called the Longhorn killer."

No. I died already.

His spinning mind drank the bitter blood.

I'm in hell for my sins.

"But let me repeat, you are no longer this person.

In fact the journey here has likely burned away, so to speak, all aspects of the neural wiring...."

The voice faded in and out. Time stuttered. Consciousness hopped.

Another voice faded in. Higher pitched and glottal.

"A final sign. He has arrived."

In the center of his tunnel vision, an unknown face floated. Mottled skin. Hair sparse. Eyes missing and replaced by coarse, white disks.

"And yet he dies," said Fenn.

"You will remake him. Those remade will prepare the way for the Mother."

The tunnel narrowed to a point. Light vanished. His vision was gone.

"Mr. Mattox? Norm? Can you hear me?"

He was gone.

Hard Time, Book 3: Cult

In Book 3, **Cult**, missionaries arrive on a holy quest to fulfill their scriptures. But the desert has other plans. Will they escape with their faith, or even their lives, intact?